#13
Anaconda Adventure

Books in the
S.W.I.T.C.H. series

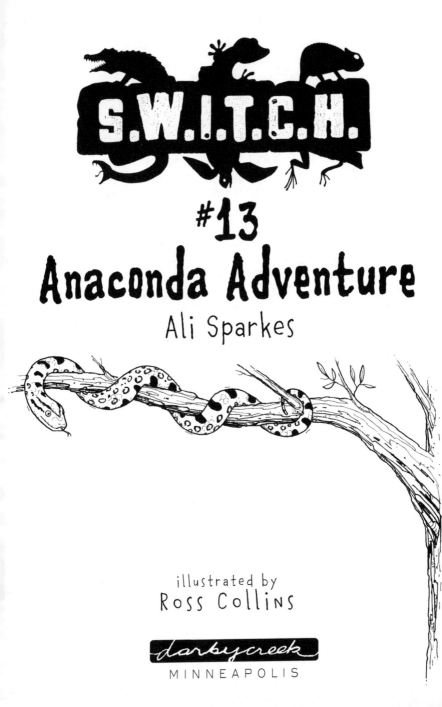

S.W.I.T.C.H.

#13
Anaconda Adventure

Ali Sparkes

illustrated by
Ross Collins

darbycreek

MINNEAPOLIS

Text © Ali Sparkes 2012
Illustrations © Ross Collins 2012

"SWITCH: Anaconda Adventure" was originally published in English in 2012
This edition is published by an arrangement with Oxford University Press.

Copyright © 2014 by Darby Creek

Darby Creek
A division of Lerner Publishing Group, Inc.
241 First Avenue North
Minneapolis, MN 55401 U.S.A.

For reading levels and more information, look up this title at
www.lernerbooks.com.

Main body text set in ITC Goudy Sans Std. 14/19.
Typeface provided by Monotype Typography.

Library of Congress Cataloging-in-Publication Data
Sparkes, Ali.
    Anaconda adventure / by Ali Sparkes ; illustrated by Ross Collins.
        pages   cm. — (S.W.I.T.C.H. ; #13)
    Summary: At the zoo, twins Josh and Danny willingly try out Petty Pott's
new REPTOSWITCH formula and enjoy being snakes until they are spotted
by a group of girls on a field trip, including their camp friend, Charlie.
    ISBN 978-1-4677-2116-5 (lib. bdg. : alk. paper)
    ISBN 978-1-4677-2415-9 (eBook)
    [1. Zoos—Fiction. 2. Anaconda—Fiction. 3. Brothers—Fiction.
4. Twins—Fiction. 5. Science fiction.] I. Collins, Ross, illustrator. II. Title.
PZ7.S73712Anf 2014
    [Fic]—dc23
                                                            2013019717

Manufactured in the United States of America
1 – SB – 12/31/12

For Tobey Cole

With grateful thanks to
John Buckley and Tony Gent of
Amphibian and Reptile Conservation
for their hot-blooded guidance on
S.W.I.T.C.H.'s cold-blooded reptile heroes

Danny and Josh and Petty

Josh and Danny might be twins, but they're NOT the same. Josh loves getting his hands dirty and learning about nature. Danny thinks Josh is a nerd. Skateboarding and climbing are way cooler! And their next-door neighbor, Petty, is only interested in one thing . . . her top secret S.W.I.T.C.H. potion.

Danny

- FULL NAME: Danny Phillips
- AGE: eight years
- HEIGHT: taller than Josh
- FAVORITE THING: skateboarding
- WORST THING: creepy-crawlies and tidying
- AMBITION: to be a stuntman

Josh

- FULL NAME: Josh Phillips
- AGE: eight years
- HEIGHT: taller than Danny
- FAVORITE THING: collecting insects
- WORST THING: skateboarding
- AMBITION: to be an entomologist

Petty

- FULL NAME: Petty Hortense Potts
- AGE: none of your business
- HEIGHT: head and shoulders above every other scientist
- FAVORITE THING: S.W.I.T.C.H.ing Josh & Danny
- WORST THING: evil ex-friend Victor Crouch
- AMBITION: adoration and recognition as the world's most genius scientist (and for the government to say sorry!)

Contents

Getting Legless

"Slithery, slithery, slithery . . ." Petty Potts pushed her face up against the glass, steaming it up with her breath and bending her nose sideways.

"She's going wrong again," muttered Danny.

"Ahem! Who's *she*?" demanded Petty Potts, stepping away from the glass and shoving her thick spectacles up the bridge of her nose so she could glare at him. "The cat's mother? I was merely trying to build the excitement."

"You don't need to build any excitement!" Josh pointed to the enormous snake on the other side of the glass. "You're just about to S.W.I.T.C.H. Danny and me into one of *those*. It doesn't get more exciting than that!"

"Although we're not sure why you want to do

it *here*," Danny added. They were in the reptile
house at The Wilderness Zoological Park.
"I mean—surely it would be safer to do this
S.W.I.T.C.H. in the lab?"

"It would," Petty said. "But I'm working on
a new theory. Will your behavior patterns be
affected if you S.W.I.T.C.H. in proximity to a real
snake?"

Josh and Danny stared through the glass and
shivered with excitement . . . and a little fear. On
the far side, a yellow and black scaly face rose
up, staring back at them through almond-shaped

eyes. A black forked tongue waved in the air, trying to scent them.

"A yellow anaconda," read Danny, peering at the little information plaque next to the display. "Grows up to two or three yards in length and eats birds, reptiles and mammals. Non venomous. Kills prey by constriction. Not large enough to kill humans. Aaaw!" He turned to Petty. "I want to be large enough to kill humans! Why can't I be large enough to kill humans? It's not fair."

Josh thwacked the back of his twin brother's head with a rolled-up Wilderness Zoological Park souvenir guide, briefly flattening Danny's spiky blond hair. "You're not planning to kill any humans, are you? So it's not really a problem!"

"I know . . ." pouted Danny. "I'd just like to know we could if we wanted to . . ."

"Which is precisely why you're getting this S.W.I.T.C.H. spray," Petty said, holding out a small, white plastic bottle with a spray nozzle on the top. The letters "Y A" for yellow anaconda were written on it in permanent marker. "I do have a green anaconda spray too, and they're the huge, human-eating size. But that's for later. For now, I don't want you getting overexcited and deciding to crush me to death on a whim. And in any case, you're only going to be S.W.I.T.C.H.ed for half a minute. This bottle has a very precise spray button, and I've calculated the dose for exactly thirty seconds and no more."

When Josh and Danny had first been S.W.I.T.C.H.ed, it was by accident—into house spiders. It had been utterly terrifying to be the unwitting guinea pigs for Petty's Serum Which Instigates Total Cellular Hijack—and it would never have happened at all if Piddle, their dog, (named after a rather unfortunate habit he had when he got excited) hadn't run into their neighbor's back garden. It was while rescuing him that they'd stumbled into Petty's secret underground laboratory—and right into a jet spray of S.W.I.T.C.H.

Now, months later, it was hard to imagine how they'd resisted getting involved with Petty's S.W.I.T.C.H. Project. Since they'd helped her find the missing code to the Reptile S.W.I.T.C.H. formula, they'd been more and more excited about taking part in the experiments. Being S.W.I.T.C.H.ed into reptiles was going to be amazing!

Even so, today Josh felt a twinge of worry—a zoological park was a bit public for a brand new S.W.I.T.C.H.. "Are you sure about this?" he asked Petty. "It will definitely only last thirty seconds?"

"Certain!" Petty said. "Now—check there's nobody coming and we'll give it a blast." While Josh and Danny poked their heads out past the door of the reptile house—a humid hexagonal building filled with large glass-fronted displays containing all kinds of exotic cold-blooded creatures—Petty put her bag down on a table in the center of the room. It was used as an education center too, so there were tables and chairs and benches along one wall.

"Nope—nobody around," Danny said, coming back in. "Good thing we're off school on a teacher training day. This place would be full of kids on the weekend."

"Yes—but school groups sometimes come in too," Petty said. "And I saw one back by the

15

entrance gate. Still—if nobody was anywhere near the bottom of the path, we know we have a minute or more. It's a long walk up here. So—climb on the table please. As soon as you S.W.I.T.C.H., pay attention to the yellow anaconda. Look at it. And let it look at you. I will be filming to see if there are any differences in behavior. And you'll S.W.I.T.C.H. back in half a minute—so no chance to get chummy with my windpipe!"

Danny and Josh sat cross-legged on the table, grinning with excitement. They'd been looking forward to this moment for weeks and weeks— ever since they'd found the last REPTOSWITCH cube and Petty had begun working on the new formula. Josh decided to stop worrying and just have fun.

He fixed his blue eyes on Petty and said, "Ready!"
Petty sprayed him in one short burst—then Danny.

Three seconds later, two yellow anacondas
were coiling on the table, black and yellow scales
gleaming in the soft light, diamond-shaped heads
swaying back and forth and black forked tongues
flickering in the air.

"YESSSSSSSSSSSSS!" hissed Danny.

"This is SSSSSSSSSSO cool!" hissed Josh.

Although it was weird to have no arms or legs,
Josh could feel the immense strength and agility
of his sleek body. He lifted his head, feeling the
muscles contract and relax in waves just under his
beautiful gleaming scales, and rose up majestically
to stare at Danny.

"Look at my toooongue!" Danny poked out his
forked tongue and waved it around. It was like a
tiny snake in itself—strong and agile.

"We're quite small," Josh said, eyeing his tail.
"About three feet, I think. Not big enough to kill
much more than a mouse. Oooh—quick—look
at whatsisface! We've only got about ten seconds
left."

Whatsisface, the real anaconda, was now staring at them through the glass with interest. He'd risen up higher, and his tongue was going crazy . . . but he couldn't hope to get much information through it, thought Josh. Not with that thick glass between him and them. Petty's experiment would have worked better if he and Danny had been able to get in with the other snakes, behind the glass. But as anacondas occasionally ate each other, it was probably just as well they hadn't.

"How are we talking this time?" asked Danny, writhing around in great excitement, his scales rubbing together with a soft whispery noise.

"Oh, like most reptiles—through scent and body language and a bit of hissing," explained Josh. "You're smelling through your tongue!" Josh was mad about wildlife and knew a lot of this stuff. "Ooh—I can't wait to do this back in Petty's garden. We can go into the stream at the back. You know anacondas are brilliant swimmers, don't you? They spend more time in water, in the wild, than on land!"

"Hmmm—but will she let us?" asked Danny. "Since she's moved her secret lab to the attic above Princessland, she's not doing any experiments in the old lab at home anymore, is she? In case government spies are watching her!"

"Well . . . we'll just have to go off down the park and have a swim in the lake," Josh said.

"Um . . . shouldn't we have S.W.I.T.C.H.ed back by now?" asked Danny. "It's been more than thirty seconds, hasn't it?"

Josh turned to look at Petty and saw that she was legging it out of the room. "WRONG SPRAY BOTTLE!" she shouted, as she went. "GETTING

ANTIDOTE FROM CAR! HIDE!" The last they saw
of her was the back of her purple beanie hat—and
even that looked quite panicky.

"Oh, great!" Danny stared back at Josh. "She's
done a runner!"

"We'll be fine." Josh gulped. "She'll be back soon.
We just have to hide in case anyone else comes in."

The real anaconda was swaying about even higher
now, behind the glass. Its eyes glimmered, and its
tongue was still dancing. It seemed to be laughing
at them.

"Come on . . ." Josh said. "Get down!"

They worked their way down the table legs,
coiling around them to reach the floor. Under the
table wasn't a good hiding place. They might easily
be seen by someone walking in. "This way!" Danny

hissed, sliding across the cold tiles and under one of the long wooden benches against one wall of the reptile house. Soon Josh and Danny were hiding in the shadows.

"She won't be long," Josh said. "She'll be back any minute. It'll be fine! Hey—I can feel her vibrations now." And he *could* feel the vibration of steps back up the path outside. Of course, snakes were excellent at picking up vibrations—sometimes from far, far away. Josh knew that it was one of the things that helped them hunt.

"Erm . . . isn't that quite a *lot* of vibrations for one genius scientist?" Danny queried.

And then the door crashed open, and two dozen sets of feet pounded into the room.

And not one of them was Petty's.

In the Bag

Josh and Danny flattened themselves right against the wall as the stampede thundered across the floor. The shoes were mostly black and shiny with silver buckles across white, lace-trimmed socks. They crashed around in all directions . . . some rushing toward the glass displays, some coming to rest by the tables, and some, alarmingly, stomping down right by the benches.

"Girls! Girls!" called a shrill voice. "Don't forget to make notes on your worksheets!"

It was a school group. A girls' school group. Keeping his head low, Danny could see girls in maroon and gray checked skirts, white blouses, and maroon blazers—and straw hats!

"What are we going to do?" he whispered to Josh.

"Just keep very still!" Josh whispered back.

"They won't stay long. There're loads of other things to see around the park. They'll only be here five minutes. And Petty will be back any time . . ."

Danny kept very still. He found it quite easy to keep his reptilian body motionless. And of course, snakes were good at that. Josh had told him they could keep incredibly still—and then strike, out of nowhere. But he couldn't help his tongue continually sliding out from his lipless mouth and flickering in the air. Gathering information through scent glands, according to Josh.

The noise of the girls was head-splitting. They were constantly babbling and squeaking and even screaming when they saw a reptile they didn't like the look of. But one girl was sitting quietly on the bench just above them. Her feet were not moving. Her shoes were spattered with mud. She didn't say anything to any of the others.

"Righto, girls!" said the teacher. "Let's have our packed lunches while we're here. Sit down and get your food out." There was another short stampede as the girls rushed to get a decent seat.

"Move up, new girl!" said one of them in a

sneery voice, and the girl sitting above Josh and Danny was shoved abruptly along the bench. She didn't say anything, but she lifted her muddy shoe and stepped down hard on the shiny neat shoe of the girl who'd arrived next to her. The new arrival screamed in a very melodramatic way. "Miss Biffle! Miiiss! Charlotte just stamped on my foot! Charlotte just broke my toes! Miiiss!"

"Shove me again and I'll make you some toe jam," promised Charlotte in a sweet voice. Josh and Danny snorted with amusement. They liked the sound of Charlotte.

But the teacher wasn't paying attention amid the racket of twenty-four girls settling down to a picnic. Above their heads Danny and Josh could hear the pop, crackle, and rasp of plastic tubs opening and food being freed from paper or tinfoil.

"Oooh, look!" said the crushed toe victim. "Charlotte's got Marmite on white bread again! Is that all you can eat, Charlotte? Oh—and a bag of corn puffs! What a lunch! So yeasty and cheesy . . ."

Several girls tittered around the room.

"Or is that just your disgusting socks?" went on the voice.

There was a small crackle of a packet and then a loud scream. "Miiiiiss! Miss Biffle!" Amid the new screaming there was also laughter—hoots of it. "Miiiiisss! Charlotte just stuck two corn puffs up my nose!"

"It's a good look, Isobella," Charlotte said. "They match your eyes." More girls laughed. It looked as if this Charlotte was winning the match.

Josh and Danny were laughing helplessly too, their scaly heads rocking from side to side. They only wished they could have seen it. Miss Biffle called for calm and told Charlotte off, and things settled down again.

"I'll get you back for that!" Isobella whispered. "Just you wait!"

"Whenever you're ready," Charlotte said.

A few seconds later an orange rolled under the bench. Then a face with a neat blond fringe and two wide gray eyes peered into their hiding place.

And that's when Isobella really started screaming.

"AAAAAAAH! SNAKES! SNAKES! MISS! THERE ARE SNAKES!!"

Immediately there was a mad cacophony of shrieks and yelps, and all the feet were running to the far end of the room and jumping up on chairs and tables. "What do you mean, Isobella?" bellowed Miss Biffle. "Of course there are snakes in here! It's a reptile house!"

"No! Escaped snakes! Under the bench!" More hysterical shrieking shook the air, and the teacher walked hesitantly across to the bench and peered under. She gasped and called out, "Stay back, everyone! Stay back! Isobella—Jemima! Run and

find a member of the zoo staff right away."

"What do we do now?" hissed Danny, the cool blood in his veins pumping hard around his lengthy body as panic started to creep through him.

"Just keep really still!" hissed back Josh. "And stop hissing!" It was all he could think of . . . and it wasn't much. Any minute a zookeeper would be along with a snake hook and a bag—and they'd be caught! Unless they S.W.I.T.C.H.ed back to boys first—and that would also be a catastrophe. How would they ever explain themselves? Petty Potts—of course—was nowhere to be seen.

"What is going on?" A new voice rang out amid all the squeaks and shrieks.

"Oh, Miss Butcher!" breathed Miss Biffle. "Thank goodness you've come! It's snakes! Under the bench! We're waiting for the staff to come and catch them."

"Well—shouldn't you be evacuating the girls?" demanded Miss Butcher.

"Oh, yes—I suppose so," agreed Miss Biffle. "Come on, girls—we'd better wait outside."

And the girls all ran for the door in a heaving mob.

"Girls! Girls!" called Miss Butcher. "Don't push! It's unladylike. Charlotte! Why are you coming back inside? You've only just gone out!"

"I forgot something, Miss," came back Charlotte's increasingly familiar voice. And then she was running across the room right toward the spot where Danny and Josh were frozen under the bench. "My bag!"

"Don't!" shrieked Miss Biffle. "That's right where the snakes are!"

But Charlotte not only grabbed her bag, she also tipped it over and scrabbled around by the bench, scooping all her bits and pieces back into it. "It's OK!" she called back. "They're only small ones. And they're not venomous—they're constrictors. And . . . I have to be honest . . . um . . . they're not real."

"I beg your pardon!" squawked Miss Biffle.

Then the girl whispered under the bench. "Quick! Get into my bag! NOW!"

Josh and Danny gaped at each other and then slid right into the open neck of the duffel bag—passing, as they did, some long, thin, rubbery things.

Charlotte dug her hand back into her bag the second they were both coiled up inside it, amid her pens, paper, and crumpled-up sweet wrappers. She pulled out the long, thin, rubbery things.

"Josh!" whispered Danny. "Did you see that? Did you?"

"Yes! But shhhhh! We have to stay quiet!" urged Josh.

Danny had seen two amazing things. One was that they had just been replaced, under the bench, by two rubber toy snakes.

The second was that he knew who Charlotte was. And they could not have asked for a better rescuer.

"Charlotte Wexford—what ARE you talking about?" shouted Miss Butcher. "I demand you tell me this instant!"

"Well . . ." sighed Charlotte. Through a gap at the top of the bag Josh and Danny saw her reach under the bench and pull out the two fake snakes. "It was kind of a joke . . . that's all. I didn't think everyone would freak out quite so much."

"You mean to tell me," spluttered Miss Butcher, "that you came in here, planning to play a trick on everyone, deliberately, calculatingly, smuggling in two rubber snakes in your bag?"

"Yeah—*rubber* ones!" Charlotte said, picking up her bag and putting it carefully over her shoulder. "I mean—I'm not going to go around with *real* snakes in my bag, am I?"

In her bag, two real snakes grinned at each other.

"I can't believe it!" whispered Danny. "It's Charlie!"

Charlie About

The face that peered down at them through the opening in the duffel bag had big brown eyes, a cloud of curly black hair, and a naughty grin that Josh and Danny had last seen at their adventure camp in the summer holidays. Charlie was the only friend they had who knew about S.W.I.T.C.H.

"Josh! Danny! The teachers have put me back on the bus as a punishment," Charlie called in a low voice. "You can come out now! I mean . . . it *is* you two, isn't it?"

"Yess!" hissed back Danny. "But how on earth did you know?"

Of course, Charlie couldn't work out what he was saying, but she seemed to guess. "I've got no idea what you two are doing in the middle of my school trip, S.W.I.T.C.H.ed into snakes," she went on. "And you nearly got completely caught out this time! The keeper was just running up from the bottom of the path when we all came out of the reptile house."

Charlie giggled. "Then I saw her! Petty Potts! Standing there on the path with a little white S.W.I.T.C.H. spray bottle in her hands, looking at us as if her underwear had just caught fire! And in that second I realized what was happening. A pair of escaped snakes under the bench! Petty Potts in the area! It had to be you two! And so I had to think fast—really fast! And guess what? I'd just bought these rubber snakes from the gift shop! Of course, they've been confiscated now," she sighed.

"She's brilliant! Just brilliant!" Danny said. "Best girl in the world!"

"Danny," Josh said. "We'd better get out of this bag. We could S.W.I.T.C.H. back at any minute. It's a nice bag but I don't want to end up wearing it!" Josh lifted his head through the top of the bag and began to slither across Charlie's arm.

"Wow! You are fab!" murmured Charlie,

running her fingers along the smooth black and yellow scales that formed a three-pronged arrow shape on his head. Josh soon slid across to the spare seat next to her, and Danny began to wind out of the bag too. "YEE-OW!" added Charlie. With some cause. Suddenly an eight-year-old boy was sprawling across her lap.

"Ahem. Sorry," Danny said, scrambling off, looking a little pink.

"Thank you!" Josh said, also back in boy form now. "So much! If you hadn't come along and swapped those toy snakes for us, we'd be in captivity now. Behind glass. Probably with one of the real anacondas deciding which one of us to crush first."

"Glad to be of service." Charlie beamed. "After all—you helped *me* out back at summer camp. I still can't believe I got to be a frog! It was the best thing ever!"

"What happened to your hair?" Danny asked. In summer camp, where he and Josh had first met Charlie, she'd had her black hair in many long beaded braids.

"Oh—that!" Charlie tugged at the bloom of frizzy black curls with a frown. "St. Gwendoline's doesn't allow hair with beads in. I had to have them all taken out—and now I have to brush my hair every day! Can you believe it? Me?"

"It still looks cool," Danny said. "But you don't like St. Gwendoline's much, do you?"

Charlie shrugged. "Mom thought it might calm me down, you know . . . being in a fancy school where you have to wear a proper uniform and all that. With strict teachers and . . . eurgh! Straw hats! But it's not that bad. Most of the girls are all right . . . apart from Isobella!"

"Did you really stick corn puffs up her nose?" chuckled Danny.

"She had it coming," sniffed Charlie. "Next time it'll be Pringles down her pants!"

"We should probably try to find Petty," sighed Josh when they'd all finished laughing. "She'll be getting worried."

"Doesn't stop her, though, does it?" Charlie said. "What have you been S.W.I.T.C.H.ed into since we were all frogs in the summer?"

Danny counted on his fingers, "Um . . . common lizard and sand lizard . . . chameleons . . . leatherback turtles and—just last week—geckos!"

"Geckos!" echoed Charlie, her face awash with first awe and then envy. "Ooooh! I would *love* to be a gecko! Did you walk up walls?"

"Yup!" Josh said. "And across ceilings!"

"I have got to get some of that spray from Petty!" Charlie said. "It's brilliant that you found those cubes and got the REPTOSWITCH formula for her."

"That's not all we've found," Josh said, more seriously now. He and Danny exchanged glances.

"What? What's going on?" asked Charlie.

"We've been getting marbles . . ." explained Danny. "Or rather, clues to find them. Sent to us or delivered in some way."

"Who from?" asked Charlie.

"That's just it . . . we don't know. We call him—or her—The Mystery Marble Sender," Josh said. "We've followed the clues and found four of them now."

Charlie shrugged. "Well . . . marbles are no big deal. I've got bags of them at home. Why would anyone bother?"

"They're not ordinary marbles," Josh said. "They contain code, like the REPTOSWITCH cubes. Petty Potts's code!"

Charlie looked confused. "Umm . . . so is *Petty Potts* sending the clues to find S.W.I.T.C.H. marbles to you? And . . . er . . . why?"

40

"No!" Danny said. "She says she isn't. She's just as confused as we are. She recognized the marble we showed her right away but said she'd forgotten she'd made it. We think it's for a kind of MAMMALSWITCH."

Charlie's eyes widened. "What . . . like tigers and elephants and all that?" she murmured.

"Maybe," Josh said. "But there are still two more to find before we can give Petty the whole code— and in the meantime . . . it's kind of creepy. Who's sending them to us? And why? What do they know about S.W.I.T.C.H. and Petty? And what are they going to do next?"

"Whoever it was even followed us on holiday to Cornwall," added Danny. "They sent us a clue on a parachute! We found that marble in a ruined fort just off the coast."

"Ooooow! I wish I'd been there!" Charlie folded her arms and huffed. "You two have the best fun!"

"Yeah—and nearly get ripped apart by hungry owls, dropped from a great height, drowned while trapped in fishing net, forced to be gladiators by crazed princesses . . ." listed Danny.

"Sheeesh!" Charlie raised an eyebrow. "Crazed princesses . . . that does sound scary."

"Thing is . . . whoever this is . . . are they watching us now?" murmured Josh.

They were all quiet for a while, glancing around them uneasily, and then Charlie went on, "Anyway . . . is there any chance Petty might let me have just a little gecko S.W.I.T.C.H. spray? Or snake S.W.I.T.C.H. spray? I'd love to be a snake! I'd love to be a DUCK!"

"A duck?" Josh looked confused. "You want to be a duck?"

"NO! DUCK!" yelled Charlie. "Miss Butcher's coming!"

Josh and Danny threw themselves into the aisle, crawled at top speed toward the back of the bus and hid behind the seats—just in time. The bus door opened and Miss Butcher strode in.

"Charlotte Wexford!" she barked. "I'm afraid you have to come with me. As much as I would like to leave you here on your own all afternoon, we are heading down to the river walk now, and health and safety rules mean I can't leave you unsupervised. Although it's certainly what you deserve for your appalling behavior."

"Yes, Miss Butcher," Charlie said. She didn't sound remotely troubled.

"You can wipe that cheerful look off your face, too," snapped Miss Butcher. "You needn't think, just because I have to bring you along, that you're about to have any fun. You'll stay right between Miss Biffle and me the whole time. And I will call your mother into the school to discuss your future just as soon as we get back today."

Charlie sighed. "Yes, Miss Butcher," she said, getting to her feet and managing to sound a bit less chipper.

"I really don't know what gets into you," muttered the teacher, stepping out of the bus. "You're easily as clever as the other girls, but you're always so naughty."

"I'm not really naughty," Charlie was saying as the bus door closed. "I'm just misunderstood . . ."

Danny got up from behind the seat and peeped out of the window as the teacher and their friend walked away. "It's not fair," he said. "Charlie got herself into big trouble—just to save you and me! And now she's going to get into even more trouble when they call her mom in. What if she gets expelled? It'll be our fault—and Petty's fault too."

"There must be something we can do," Josh said. "But I can't think what. We can't tell them that Charlie was actually saving our lives. Nobody would believe us."

"No . . ." sighed Danny. "Being S.W.I.T.C.H.ed is amazing, like having super powers. But how much good is it? Charlie's doomed. There's nothing we can do . . ."

Pocket Problem

Petty was worried. Really worried. Josh and Danny might imagine that she was a heartless scientist, obsessed only with her own success, but she really did care about what happened to them. After all . . . who else was going to help her with her experiments if Josh and Danny got eaten?

Of course, if they were still in anaconda form, it was highly unlikely that anything *would* try to eat them . . . but a panicky member of the public might stamp on them, or the keeper might catch them and put them in with another constrictor and it might . . . Petty shuddered, imagining two Josh- and Danny-shaped bumps moving slowly down the body of the huge green anaconda she'd seen in the reptile house. This breed had been known to eat each other—*and* small humans. So, S.W.I.T.C.H.ed or unS.W.I.T.C.H.ed, Josh and Danny could be lunch.

There had been no sign of them in the reptile house, and the keeper, coming out past her as she went in, had not been carrying a bag of captured snakes. So where had Josh and Danny gone? She'd searched for them in the zoo shop, the café, even in the small Chatz TV marquee which was set up near the penguins, recording some kind of wildlife program. Josh would love that! But he wasn't there.

She could see that group of schoolchildren—an expensive girls' school by the look of the straw hats—heading along the path toward the river. She hurried toward them and called out, "Have any of you seen two boys—blond—twins— about your age?"

The girls looked at each other and then back at her. Some of them shrugged and several of them giggled. "I love her hat!" snickered one girl with a shiny fair bob of hair and a superior expression. "It's soooo antique."

Petty narrowed her eyes at the girl as she patted her battered beanie. "Well, I'd offer to swap it for yours," she said. "Except your head is far too small. Such a tragedy, an undersized brain!"

"Well! I've never been so insulted!" gasped the girl.

"Really?" said Petty. "I'm surprised nobody's made the effort."

Another girl, with a cloud of black curls and dark brown eyes, hooted with laughter and gave Petty a little wave as the party was hurried along the path by its two guardian teachers. The laughing girl was walking close to the teachers. They were deep in conversation with each other and paying no attention to her as she turned back to Petty and motioned urgently at her . . . as if she wanted Petty to follow.

Uncertainly, Petty followed, keeping a short distance from the school party. Then the girl dropped down and started to fiddle with her shoe. Her teachers, calling out to their pupils ahead to make notes of the trees along the river, didn't notice.

Petty caught up, and the girl immediately bounced up on her feet and gave her a friendly punch on the shoulder. "Petty! It's meeee! Charlie!"

"Good gracious!' Petty squinted through her smeary glasses. "So it is! Whatever happened to your hair?"

"Never mind that now," Charlie said. "We haven't got long! Josh and Danny are OK. I rescued them in my bag. I had to leave them on the school bus, though, hiding." She waved back toward the zoo parking lot.

"Thank heavens for that!" sighed Petty, turning to go.

"But wait . . . can't I have just a little S.W.I.T.C.H. spray before you go? Pleeeeease?" Charlie gave Petty the big eyes treatment. "I mean . . . I did just save Josh's and Danny's lives! Probably!"

"And I thank you very much," Petty said. "But I don't hand out S.W.I.T.C.H. like candy, you know. Well . . . I did once, but that was a bad idea . . ."

"But I'd be ever so careful!" insisted Charlie. "I would never use it in public or . . ."

"Charlie! You are a first-rate girl, and I would love to get you on the S.W.I.T.C.H. Project," Petty said. "But I'm not handing over S.W.I.T.C.H. spray to you just for fun. You know how dangerous it is. Didn't you nearly end up as a heron's breakfast last time? No—I'm sorry, but that's that."

And Petty turned on her heel and fell over.

"Oooh—these stupid woodland paths!" she snapped, as Charlie helped her to her feet. "What's wrong with a nice bit of tarmac?" And, carefully stepping over the tree root that had tripped her, Petty hurried away.

Charlie was about to call after her. She really *was*. Because a small white bottle with a squirty spray button on it had fallen out of Petty's coat pocket as she tripped. Charlie really *wouldn't* have kept it if Miss Butcher hadn't, at that moment, turned around and bellowed at her from farther along the path.

"Charlotte Wexford! Come here AT ONCE!"

"Oh, well," muttered Charlie, slipping the bottle into her blazer pocket. "I'll be able to mail it to her. Probably."

Josh and Danny hit the emergency exit button and got off the bus at the back, without getting noticed. Happily, it didn't set off any kind of alarm. A minute later they found Petty Potts stomping up to the parking lot, muttering to herself.

"It's OK—we're safe," called Josh.

"You'll never guess what!" called Danny, as they reached Petty on the path to the parking lot. "We were rescued by—"

"Charlie Wexford!" Petty said. She seemed to be turning out her pockets. "Yes, I know. I just met her on the river path. And I do believe the little lightfingers pickpocketed my S.W.I.T.C.H. spray!"

"What—Charlie? Steal? She wouldn't do that!" Josh said.

"Don't be so sure," sniffed Petty. "She's a very determined young lady, and she wanted some S.W.I.T.C.H."

"Even so," Danny said. "Charlie's all right!"

"I didn't say she wasn't all right," Petty said. "I've been known to steal things myself when it was desperately important. But not just for fun! Come on—we have to find her and get that spray back. There's been far too much upset today. Why on earth did you think it would be a good idea for us to try out a S.W.I.T.C.H. at the zoo?"

"We didn't!" Josh said, stonily. "You did!"

"I did not!" Petty turned and stomped back into the park again, and they hurried along with her.

"You did!" Danny said. "You said you wanted to see how S.W.I.T.C.H.ing near real snakes affected us."

"Yes, of course I did!" Petty said. "So why did you say I didn't?"

"Petty, you could have some amazing arguments just on your own," sighed Josh.

They saw Charlie, at a distance, down by the river with the other St. Gwendoline's students following the river wildlife walk. "We'll run ahead," Danny said. "Make sure she doesn't get away!" He and Josh took off, leaving Petty grumbling as she marched on after them, looking out for trippy tree roots.

"Get that S.W.I.T.C.H. spray back!" she called after them. "Charlie has no idea how dangerous it can be! If she uses it, there will be trouble. Desperate trouble . . ."

Desperate Trouble

Charlie caught up with the others as they reached the river, which wiggled through the many acres of the zoological park, passing the enclosures of giraffe and rhino and ostrich. At this end, though, it had left the exotic animals behind and was rushing into the countryside. Little information posts along the path offered tips on where to spot woodpeckers, kingfishers, and foxes.

They stopped near an arched stone bridge that spanned the river. Below, on the near side, the water tumbled over some rocks in a small, fast waterfall, and on the far side the current moved much faster as the river deepened and flowed on downstream. There were warning signs that nobody should swim in it.

"I haven't got a small head—have I?" Isobella was demanding.

Her two best friends, Lucy and Jemima, chorused, "Of course not!"

"But that horrid, ugly old witch lady said I had!" pouted Isobella, taking off her straw hat and patting her hair anxiously. "She said I had an undersized brain!"

"She got *that* right," muttered Charlie.

Isobella spun around and glared at her. "What would you know, Wexford?" she spat. Then she turned back to her friends. "It's horrible! Our teachers should complain to the park staff. It's not right for ugly old witch ladies to go around picking on well brought up young ladies!"

Charlie snorted as she climbed up onto the parapet of the bridge. "Oh, give it a rest, Isobella. Don't be such a wuss."

Isobella gasped again. "Who are you calling a wuss?" she hissed.

"Um . . . that would be you!" Charlie said, walking along the parapet, holding her arms out wide for balance.

"I suppose you think you're so brave!" sneered Isobella. "Just because you can walk along the wall of a bridge!"

"Nope. Just very good at it," Charlie said. "I do gymnastics, remember? I have a good sense of balance." She stood on one leg to prove it.

"Oh you really think you're it!" Isobella stared with her hands on her hips for a moment, and then she scrambled up on the parapet too.

"Whoa!" Charlie said. "Don't do that! It's dangerous."

"But you're doing it!" Isobella said.

"Yes! Because I'm *good* at this! You're not!"
Charlie said, alarmed. "You can't even balance
along the curb! Get off, Isobella! Look—I'm
getting down now. It's too dangerous for me."
And she hurriedly got back down onto the path.
She glanced around, hoping for a chance that one
of the teachers would turn and make Isobella get
down—but neither did. They were studying tree
bark.

"Izzy! Don't!" whimpered Lucy.

"You'll fall!" warned Jemima.

But Isobella was smirking and throwing her arms
out wide and walking, rather shakily, along the top

of the narrow stone wall. Ten feet below her, the river churned and flowed at high speed.

"Isobella! Please!" Charlie gave up trying to be cool as the girl wobbled along to the middle of the parapet.

"You think I can't make it across, don't you?" Isobella said, glancing defiantly at Charlie.

"No! I know you can. I'm sorry—I was just showing off," gabbled Charlie. "You're better than I am . . . just . . . get down!"

"I'll get down when I'm good and ready!" snapped Isobella, waving her arms about.

And then she fell off.

Josh and Danny were just running up to Charlie to quietly get back the S.W.I.T.C.H. spray when something astonishing happened. One minute Charlie was walking along the top of the parapet (which did not surprise Josh and Danny one bit) and the next minute another girl had climbed up, wobbled along it, and then fallen off.

The girls watching her, Charlie included, were so shocked they didn't even scream. They just gaped and then ran to the wall and peered over.

Josh and Danny arrived next to them in time to see a straw hat bob up on the surface and spin away downstream. Charlie turned to them, her eyes wide. "She fell!" she whispered. "She FELL!" The other girls had begun to react now. They ran to the teachers, screaming.

"I'm going after her!" Charlie said, hauling herself up on the parapet. "It's my fault!"

"Charlie—no!" hissed Danny. "It's too dangerous!" And as he said this he saw the blond-haired girl whizzing away downstream, her upturned face pink and shocked. "You'll never catch up with her and save her! None of us could. We'd need to be superhuman!"

Josh caught his breath and then plunged his hand into Charlie's blazer pocket. He brought out the S.W.I.T.C.H. bottle. It was different from the one Petty had used on them earlier—it had the letters G A on it. Josh knew exactly what those letters stood for.

He grabbed Charlie's and Danny's hands and dragged them around the far end of the bridge and down the steep woody slope to the river. Hidden by trees and bushes, Josh knew what they had to do. "Superhuman, no," he said. "But super-reptile, yes!" And he sprayed Danny and Charlie and himself.

Seconds later, three enormous green anacondas slid into the river and began to swim downstream.

63

Current Fun

Josh couldn't believe how fast he was moving. He seemed to have become part of the river—his long, muscular body rippling through the fast-flowing water. His eyes and nostrils were positioned on his head at just the right place to stay clear of the bubbling, churning surface. Water weed and bits of twig and leaf rafted along beside him. A low branch touched the surface, speeding towards his head, and he instinctively ducked under. At once his world went pale green, and a strange booming gurgle resounded through his head. Then—three seconds later—he was back on the surface.

"Where is she?" he heard Charlie shout.

"I can see her!" Josh called back, although he couldn't see Isobella that well. He could, however, smell her—and sense her body heat. She was struggling along in the water, repeatedly going under and popping up again, about thirty feet ahead of them.

"There she is!" Danny called out, spotting a flash of white lacy sock. Although, Josh realized, Danny wasn't really calling out. He was hissing a bit, yes, but like many of the creatures he and Danny had been S.W.I.T.C.H.ed into, there was other stuff going on which made up their communication: scent and body language and a bit of telepathy.

Charlie struck ahead and Josh marveled at what he saw in the water. She was bigger than he and Danny—in the wild, many female snakes were bigger than males. Charlie was at least twelve feet long! Her scales were green with black pebbly markings along the top. Josh was very glad Petty's second S.W.I.T.C.H. spray had been for a green anaconda. There was nothing in the reptile world which could swim faster down a river than a green anaconda.

They were all closing in on Isobella now—but it wasn't looking good. Just ahead of them was

66

another waterfall. From where they were swimming, Danny couldn't see the other side of the drop, but there was mist and spray rising up from it. He could hear, too, the sound of water dashing hard onto rocks.

"She'll go over the waterfall!" cried out Charlie. "Come on!" She powered through the river, carving a deep wake in the water behind her. Josh and Danny shot after her. Working his body left and right in undulating pulses, Danny felt his reptilian heart pounding. At least he thought that was his reptilian heart. He had no idea where a snake kept its heart . . .

Up ahead, Isobella was waving one feeble hand out of the water. Her face was going under again. Charlie could see her eyes were shut. *Probably just as well*, she thought. *It won't help if she sees three huge snakes coming after her!* But were they too late? With one immense effort, she lunged forward. Now Isobella was seconds away from the drop. How could Charlie save her? How was she going to grab her? Even as she thought this, Charlie opened up her powerful jaws, revealing not just fangs but two rows of needle-sharp white teeth, which pointed backward into her cavernous red mouth.

Upstream, Josh and Danny saw Charlie's jaws open in an amazingly wide gape. Josh remembered that anacondas could literally unhinge their jaws to swallow their prey whole. It was the weirdest thing he'd ever seen. A second later, Charlie had grabbed Isobella's foot in her jaws. The girl was barely conscious now as the giant snake snagged her shoe.

But the danger wasn't over. Charlie had held Isobella back from the waterfall, but she was being dragged toward it herself. Her incredibly strong, scaly body was rippling hard against the current, desperately trying to pull Isobella back upriver, but she was losing the battle. Josh and Danny had to do something—NOW!

Danny flung himself across the powerful current to the nearest bank and whipped his tail across a low branch, wrapping it around and pulling tight. And even as he did this, Josh was wrapping his tail around Danny's upper body, anchoring himself firmly with a tight coil of snake muscle.

"Behind you!" he yelled at Charlie, and she glanced back and flipped her own tail around his neck. She tightened it quickly, and the whole weight of her body—plus Isobella's—plus the strong pull of the current—dragged against Josh's neck.

"Eeeerm . . . could you just . . . loosen off a bit?" he gurgled. There was very little space left for air to get through.

"Sorry!" Charlie called back. "But we've got to get back to the bank!"

Danny was taking care of this. He wound his tail round and round the tree branch, steadily dragging himself—and Josh and Charlie and Isobella—back to the bank. A minute later they all flopped onto the ground, exhausted.

Charlie unlocked her jaws from Isobella's soggy school shoe. The thick soles had a row of punctures in them. "Good job I didn't grab her leg or her arm," she said. "I'd have bitten right through it."

"Is she alive?" Danny asked, slithering across to peer anxiously at the soaking wet schoolgirl. In response, Isobella coughed, spluttered, rolled

over and spat
water all over the
bank. Then she
slumped down
again and let out
a long sigh. Her
eyes were closed.
She seemed to be
asleep.

The three
anacondas looked
at each other.
What now?

"If she sees us
she'll freak out," Charlie said. "Probably run right
back into the river in panic. We'd better get away.
Wow! You two look amazing!" Charlie lifted her
head and swayed it from side to side, flickering a
black forked tongue out toward Josh and Danny.

"So do you," said Josh. This was truly the
most magnificent creature he'd ever been
S.W.I.T.C.H.ed into. He noticed the orangey-
yellow stripes streaking out behind Charlie's and

Danny's round dark brown eyes, and the beautiful black and yellow spots along their browny-green bodies. They were all perfect specimens. He and Danny were a little smaller and shorter than Charlie, but not by much. Josh wanted to climb up into a tree and see how strong he was. He wanted to swim some more too—a lot more! He wanted to unhinge his jaws like Charlie had and see how wide they went and what it felt like.

"We should change back any second now," he sighed. "Probably just as well—listen!" Above the hiss and bubble of the waterfall, they could hear shrill cries as Isobella's teachers rushed along the bank of the river. "We've got to go!" "Isobella! Charlie!"

called the desperate teachers, getting closer. Any minute now they could spot the astonishing sight of one half-drowned pupil and three huge anacondas coiled on the opposite bank. Josh realized it would look suspiciously as if they were planning a feast of Riverwashed Schoolgirl on a Bed of Woodland Salad. It was time to go.

"Quick—over here!" Danny said, and they all slithered away from the river and made for the cover of the wood. Shady ferns helped to hide them from view as the rescuers came running along the bank.

Charlie lost no time in heading up a tree. She wound herself around the trunk and got above ground quickly, before looping her impressive twelve-foot length along a moss-covered branch.

"Isobella! Charlotte!" called more voices. Miss Biffle and Miss Butcher were bashing their way along the river bank.

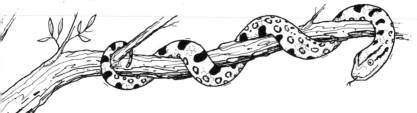

At this moment, Charlie S.W.I.T.C.H.ed back. She fell out of the tree with a splash, right into the shallows of the river.

"Ugh!" She crawled out and back over to Isobella. "Isobella!" she said, shaking the girl by the shoulder. "Izzy! Wake up! Stop looking so drowned!"

Isobella spluttered again and opened her eyes. She fluttered her lashes and whimpered. "Don't be so dramatic," said Charlie. "You only fell in a river and got swept downstream and almost over the edge of a waterfall!" She grinned. "We've had scarier experiences in the school cafeteria!"

"Charlotte! Isobella!" Shouts of delight and relief could be heard as Miss Biffle and Miss Butcher fought their way along the bank toward them. "Oh! Thank heavens!" cried Miss Biffle. "Are you all right?"

"Fine!" Charlie said. "Just went for a little swim in the river." She beamed and wrung out a soggy bunch of black curls. "Although Isobella tried to drink most of it."

Isobella sat up, looking pale and filled with

amazement. "Did you . . . just save my life?" she gasped.

Charlie shrugged. "Well, I suppose I did," she said. She'd had help, of course, but nobody would believe she'd had a couple of superhero anaconda sidekicks, so she thought it best not to mention it.

"Charlotte dived in after me and saved my life!" squeaked Isobella as soon as the teachers got there. "She's a hero! Charlotte! How can I ever thank you?"

"Ummmm . . . stop dissing my corn puffs?" suggested Charlie.

Twiglet, Anyone?

Beep. Beep. Beep. Beep.

Petty Potts reached the ash tree and peered up at Josh and Danny in its branches.

"That's a lot of top quality snakeskin you're ruining with moss stains." She waved the small, beeping, black torch-like thing at them. "At least a dozen handbags' worth." She turned off the S.W.I.T.C.H.ee detector. Its blue light went out and the beeping stopped. "Come on. Get down before you fall down. You're not even a tree-climbing breed—you shouldn't be up there! Now, I have some antidote here, but I'm not climbing up a tree with it."

Josh and Danny reluctantly slithered back down. They had enjoyed being snakes immensely. They'd both had a go at making their jaws unhinge and found that they could probably swallow a small computer console each if they wanted to. Or possibly Piddle, their dog. They had also enjoyed watching, from a distance, as Charlie was hailed a hero by the two teachers for saving Isobella's life. "Looks like she might not get expelled after all," Danny had hissed.

Petty held up the spray but paused long enough to remark, "Well! That's my best S.W.I.T.C.H. yet! I really have done wonders this time." Then she squirted them with antidote.

"Here you go," Josh said, pulling the green anaconda S.W.I.T.C.H. spray out of his pocket and handing it back to Petty. He was glad he'd shoved it into his pocket just in time, so it had safely S.W.I.T.C.H.ed too, along with all his clothes, into snakeskin, he guessed. "It was a good thing Charlie did borrow this," he told Petty. "If she hadn't had it in her pocket, we wouldn't have been able to save that girl who fell in the river."

"Really?" exclaimed Petty. "What's happened to Charlie, then?"

78

"She's S.W.I.T.C.H.ed back already and gone back with her teachers," said Danny. "Ages ago— even though we all sprayed at the same time."

"Hmmm," Petty said. "Probably to do with mass. She's female, so I'm guessing she was much larger."

"Yeah—she was huge! Amazing!" Danny marveled. "She saved that girl from going over the waterfall."

"Truly?" Petty said. "Tell me all about it!"

They told her while they made their way back to the parking lot.

"I have chocolate cake at home," Petty said, walking to her ancient station wagon. "I think chocolate cake will be just the thing to celebrate your life-saving adventure."

Petty was just about to get in when she spotted an envelope beneath one of the elderly windscreen wipers. Petty snatched it up and opened it. Then she paused, turned, and raised her shaggy gray eyebrows at Josh and Danny. Lifting the envelope, she showed them the spiky writing:

JOSH + DANNY PHILLIPS . . . AND THEIR GENIUS FRIEND.

"It seems the Mystery Marble Sender now wants me in the game too," Petty said. They all stared at each other, and Josh felt his heartbeat, not for the first time that day, skip along a little faster.

Inside was a note:

DEAR JOSH, DANNY, + PETTY
YOU'VE DONE SO WELL YOU SHOULD HAVE NO TROUBLE FINDING THIS MARBLE BEFORE YOU GO.
IT'S A LITTLE STICKY.
REMEMBER, DESTINY AWAITS!

"Is that it?" Danny said. "The clues are usually better than that!"

"A little sticky?" Josh murmured. "That could be anything!"

"Wait—there's more," Petty said. At the bottom was a PS:

DANNY ONLY. OR ELSE THE CLUES—AND YOUR JOURNEY OF DISCOVERY—END HERE.

"Me? Just me?" Danny looked worried. "But . . . I don't have any idea what the clue means. Why me?"

"Wait—there's more still," Petty said. She had flipped over the paper and now read from the back:

FISH FINGERS, PEAS, POTATOES, WART REMOVER, GET BEST YELLOW JACKET DRY CLEANED.

"Oh, that's just a bit of shopping list," Danny said. "We've had that before."

"Looks like the warts haven't cleared up yet, then," added Josh.

"OK, everyone!" Danny said. "What about the clue? What does it mean? What's sticky? And why is it just for me? What am I good at?"

Josh and Petty looked at each other and then back at the zoo. They both had the same expression on their faces. And it was not a good expression.

"Erm . . ." Josh said. "Maybe it's not to do with what you're good at, Danny."

"Well . . . why else would the Mystery Marble Sender want me to find this marble?" shrugged Danny.

"Maybe it's something you're really scared of," Josh said. "So it's more of a challenge."

Danny gulped. And then he shook his head and lifted his chin. "Nothing can be scarier than what we've had to face since we met Petty!" he declared.

"No—of course not!" Josh said with a weak grin. "Now . . . something . . . a little sticky. I have an idea."

Petty nodded. "So have I," she said. "Let's go."

They reentered the zoo for the third time that day, waving their day pass tickets at the person on the gate. Josh and Petty immediately headed for a wooden building to their left, ignoring the large pond and the wildfowl area. Danny followed them, puzzled. Something sticky, he thought, might be

frog spawn in the pond or something. But no . . .
it was autumn and you didn't get frog spawn in
the autumn. Maybe something in the visitor centre
sweet shop, then . . . but no, this was not a sweet
shop. This was . . . this was . . .

"NOOOOOOOOOO!" wailed Danny. "NOT
THE INSECT HOUSE!"

Josh and Petty each grabbed an arm and dragged
Danny inside. They knew he was scared stiff of
creepy-crawlies and would never go in on his own.
It didn't matter that he'd *been* an insect several
times; they still freaked him out. It didn't matter
that he'd even eaten quite a few insects
while he'd been S.W.I.T.C.H.ed
into a reptile or amphibian;
he'd blocked that out.

"Why are we here?" whimpered Danny, trying hard not to look at all the many-legged creepy-crawlies in their little glass displays. "There's nothing sticky about insects, is there? They're all dry and crispy and . . . eurgh!"

"Well, there's nothing sticky about most insects, true," Josh said, firmly tugging Danny along to a tall, well-lit display filled with branches and vegetation. "Except . . . these."

Danny looked through the glass and saw branches and vegetation. And twigs. And sticks. Sticks with legs. Sticks . . . with faces.

"NOOOOOOO!" he wailed. "I HATE STICK INSECTS. They're so CREEPY! NOOOO! This

can't be right! It's another kind of sticky! Toffee!
Yes! Toffee! That's sticky, isn't it? You could hide
a marble in a toffee, couldn't you? You could
definitely—"

Petty tapped him on the shoulder and pointed
into the stick insect display. In the far corner was
a small glass orb with a ribbon of purple running
through it.

It was the latest S.W.I.T.C.H. marble. Number
five.

Six or seven enormous stick insects were wiggling
about, completely surrounding the marble.

And only Danny could
get it.

Leaf Me Alone

To one side of the stick insect display, there was
a small black door with a sign that read STAFF
ONLY. This door should certainly have been
locked—but it was ajar. Petty opened it and
pulled Josh and Danny through with her before
any other visitors or staff could come in and see
them. It was gloomy behind the door. It smelled
of warm, damp vegetation. The hairs on Danny's
arms and neck stood up. His heart was racing.
He was here in the inner sanctum of the INSECT
HOUSE! It was horrific.

Petty had found the back of the stick insect
chamber and was turning a stout plastic peg
which held the access panel in place. Now she
was tilting the panel, allowing a shaft of light and
the smell of warm greenery up through it.

"Come on," Josh said. "Breathe in. You can do this."

"Look," whispered Danny, standing rigid with his fists clenched at his sides. "We're twins. Who's going to know the difference if it's you that gets the marble? The Mystery Marble Sender can't see us in here!"

Josh pointed to a little red light in the ceiling. "Security camera," he said. "I think they're watching. But you don't have to. I can get the marble. Even if the Mystery Marble Sender does see us and not send us any more clues, five marbles might be enough for Petty to carry on with creating MAMMALSWITCH."

"Yes," Petty said, peering around from the back of the stick insect display. "I might be able to work it out. After all, there were only six insect and reptile S.W.I.T.C.H. cubes. Most likely there are only six marbles, too. I might not need the last one . . ."

"But . . . if we're wrong . . ." Danny said. He took a big lungful of air and then let it out in a long, shaky breath. "No," he said. "If we don't get any more clues and you can't work out the formula,

88

I'll always know it was my fault. I'll get it."

Josh clapped his back. "I *knew* you would!"

Shaking, Danny put his hand through the open panel. In front of him was a network of branches and twigs and leaves. And some of them would be twigs and leaves. And some wouldn't . . .

"I think you're going to have to put your head through," Josh said, close behind him.

Another whimper escaped. Danny knew Josh was right. Without seeing what was below him he could be blindly swiping at stick insects.

"They're quite fragile," Josh said. "You'll hurt them—snap their legs off or something—if you grab them." He was, of course, far more worried about the stick insects than his brother.

Danny slowly pushed his head through the opening, not daring to look up in case of dangling horrors. Below him at least twenty stick insects of all sizes were clambering about. "Ooooh—they are so hoooorrible!" he moaned.

"They're fantastic!" Josh said, just behind him. "Their proper name is phasmids. They're even better at camouflage than chameleons. They live

on plants. Apart from the praying mantis variety—
that's a vicious hunter, that is. And the American
walkingstick insects can spray stuff out of their
glands that can turn you temporarily blind—I'm
going to *shut up* now . . ." tailed off Josh, realizing
how very unhelpful he was being.

"I'm still going with hoooorrible," breathed
Danny. If he could reach down through the display
without the tickle-tickle touch of one of those
hideous things against his skin, he might just have
enough courage left to knock away the thick green
one that was crouched right across the marble.

Sweat dripped
off his nose.

Slowly he moved his hand down, feeling as if he was trapped in a nightmare. Then he felt a tickle. On his left ear. He froze. "Jo-oo-oosh . . ." he squeaked. "What's on my ear?"

"Erm . . ." Josh said. "Nothing. Just a bit of leaf."

Danny didn't believe him. He started shaking badly—and then his hand bumped into a chain of three stick insects, apparently attempting a very slow trapeze act, and they tumbled right across his wrist, waggling their legs and feelers and trying to get a grip.

"Eeeeaaargh!" Danny was ready to freak out . . . but he couldn't give up! He just couldn't! He plunged his hand down and flicked the big green one off the marble. He scrabbled, moving the marble three times while yet more stick insects dropped onto his arm. And a leaf was moving down his shoulder. Only it wasn't a leaf. It was a LEAF INSECT—looking all green and leaf-shaped and innocent but with LEGS!

"Gaaaaaaaah!" Danny shot back out of the display, desperate to get the creepy-crawlies off him.

91

"STOP!" Josh yelled. "Stay ABSOLUTELY STILL!"

Danny froze. Was he about to be blinded by stick insect spit?

Josh gently collected all the creatures clinging to his brother, carefully put them back in the display, and closed the panel. "It's OK—they're all safe!" he sighed.

"THEY'RE all SAFE?" Danny spluttered. "What about ME? I could have been blinded!"

"Nah—none of these are American walkingsticks," Josh said.

"Well, thanks for telling me that NOW!" Danny stared at Josh, twitching.

"Go on," Josh said. "Freak out. Just do it quietly, OK?"

Danny freaked out. Quietly.

"Well done!" Josh said a minute later when his brother had stopped doing his little dance. "You were brilliant!" And he gave Danny a rough hug. "I mean . . . you did get it, didn't you?"

Danny grinned, held out his fist, and opened it up.

"Aha!" Petty said, her eyes gleaming in the dim light. "Number five!"

A Touch of Glass

Back in Petty's lab in the attic above Princessland (a huge shop filled with stuff for girls, which was almost as horrifying as stick insects as far as Danny was concerned), they examined the marble.

"Yes—another hologram—another bit of code," confirmed Petty, peering through her powerful microscope.

Josh and Danny took a look. The hologram this time was of a cat of some kind. A tabby . . . or a tiger. It was hard to tell.

Petty looked thoughtful. "Only one more to go," she said. "So I'm guessing our Mystery Marble Sender will reveal himself soon. And then what? This . . . feels dangerous to me. Very dangerous."

"Maybe whoever it is just wants to help," suggested Danny with a hopeful shrug.

Petty gave a hollow laugh. "Ooooh, I doubt that! Nobody ever just wants to help. Everybody's out for themselves! I learned that the hard way when my so-called best friend betrayed me and stole my work—or what he thought was my work—and burnt out my memory!"

She picked up a picture in a shattered glass frame. In it was her old friend, Victor Crouch, his arm around a younger Petty, smiling. He wore a hat but no eyebrows.

"Do you think it *is* Victor Crouch?" asked Josh. "That he survived being S.W.I.T.C.H.ed into a cockroach and then found your MAMMALSWITCH code in marbles?"

Petty stared at the picture and narrowed her eyes. "I'm not sure," she said. "It doesn't seem quite like his style. But then . . . maybe I've just forgotten what his style is."

"Well," sighed Danny. "I guess we're going to find out soon, aren't we? It won't be long now before the Mystery Marble Sender isn't a mystery anymore."

"Yes," agreed Petty. "But I have a nasty feeling we're not going to like the revelation. Go home now, both of you. Come to the house tomorrow after school. And remember, wherever you go . . . someone is watching!"

Josh and Danny were back home in time for dinner, and afterward they went down the garden with Piddle.

"It's been such a freaky few months, hasn't it?" Danny said, as they sat on the grass by the climbing frame and Piddle ran around them, trying to persuade them to throw his ball. "Nobody would ever believe what's happened to us—that we've been S.W.I.T.C.H.ed into spiders and all kinds of insects, amphibians, and reptiles."

"Nope," Josh said. "But they will one day— when Petty goes on TV. And we'll be part of it. Everyone will know then. We'll be famous."

"Maybe Charlie will be on TV with us too," Danny said. "She ought to be!"

"Danny! Josh!" called Mom from an upstairs window. "Get up here now and tidy your room! It's revolting. It's a snake pit! Really!"

Top Secret!

For Petty Potts's Eyes Only!!

SUBJECT: MARBLE NUMBER 5

Righto! Let's see if this works. Oooh! It does. I am not typing this. I'm using voice recognition software on my computer. I've always wanted to try this out. I'm speaking these words into a microphone, and they're coming out automatically across my computer screen! What fun! Now I can record my diary without using a keyboard . . .

So! Today I took Josh and Danny to the zoo to turn them into anacondas. The experiment went quite well, apart from a slight mix-up that left them as snakes for much longer than I inspected. NO—EXpected. Recognize my voice correctly, you feeble machine! Anyway, after the first S.W.I.T.C.H. they were nearly discovered by a school group—but then rescued by none other than Charlie Wexford, our friend from the summer camp! Charlie is very useful. I really must find a way to get her onto the S.W.I.T.C.H. project with Josh and Danny.

$$\frac{4 \times \pi^2}{OS-7^*} \searrow \frac{\boxed{P_2}}{0.8} \times \frac{V_6^2 \, o/q}{9.15_7^o} = \frac{4.198}{4.197} \searrow \frac{4.197}{(548)} \longrightarrow$$

Anyway—not only that—but my S.W.I.T.C.H. formula saved a life today! Josh, Danny and Charlie ended up S.W.I.T.C.H.ing into green anacondas to rescue a girl from Charlie's school after she fell into the river.

But all of this pales into insignificance against more Mystery Marble Sender news. We found another marble at the zoo! And there's something about Mystery Marble Sender's note . . . the list of shopping errands at the end . . . that has tickled my memory. The yellow jacket—it's something to do with a yellow jacket. And warts . . . I can almost see someone wearing a yellow jacket and tackling their fungal feet . . . but who? Is it my destiny to find out?

Hmmm . . . Destiny . . . Wait. Shhhh! What was that?
Who's there? Josh? Danny?
What?! Hey! What do you think you're—
NO! DOOF! GAH!
Eeeeeeeeeeeeeeeeek.
CRSSHHSZZZZ—kesheeek—ssheeeeek—sheeeeek.

Sssssssssssssssssssssssssssssssssssssssssssssssssssssssssssssssssssssssssssssssssssssssssss
ssssssssssssssssssssssssssssssssssssssssssssssssssssssssssssssssssssssssssssssssssssssssssss
ssssssssssssssssss

Recommended Reading

BOOKS

Want to brush up on your reptile knowledge?
Here's a list of books dedicated to creepy-crawlies.

Johnson, Jinny. *Animal Planet™ Wild World: An Encyclopedia of Animals*. Minneapolis: Millbrook Press, 2013.

McCarthy, Colin. *Reptile*. DK Eyewitness Books. New York: DK Publishing, 2012.

Parker, Steve. *Pond & River*. DK Eyewitness Books. New York: DK Publishing, 2011.

WEBSITES

Find out more about nature and wildlife using the websites below.

National Geographic Kids
http://kids.nationalgeographic.com/kids/
Go to this website to watch videos and read facts about your favorite reptiles and amphibians.

San Diego Zoo Kids
http://kids.sandiegozoo.org/animals
Curious to learn more about some of the coolest-looking reptiles and amphibians? This website has lots of information and stunning pictures of some of Earth's most interesting creatures.

US Fish & Wildlife Service
http://www.nwf.org/wildlife/wildlife-library
/amphibians-reptiles-and-fish.aspx
Want some tips to help you look for wildlife in your own neighborhood? Learn how to identify some slimy creatures and some scaly ones as well.

About the Author

Ali Sparkes grew up in the wilds of the New Forest, raised by sand lizards who taught her the secret language of reptiles and how to lick her own eyes.

At least, that's how Ali remembers it. Her family argues that she grew up in a house in Southampton, raised by her mom and dad, who taught her the not terribly secret language of English and wished she'd stop chewing her hair.

She once caught a slow worm. It flicked around like mad, and she was a bit scared and dropped it.

Ali still lives in Southampton, now with her husband and two sons. She likes to hang out in the nearby wildlife center spying on common lizards. The lizards are considering legal action . . .

About the Illustrator

Ross Collins's more than eighty picture books and books for young readers have appeared in print around the world. He lives in Scotland and, in his spare time, enjoys leaning backward precariously in his chair.